Welcome to ALADDIN QUIX!

If you are looking for fast, fun-to-read stories with colorful characters, lots of kid-friendly humor, easy-to-follow action, entertaining story lines, and lively illustrations, then **ALADDIN QUIX** is for you!

But wait, there's more!

If you're also looking for stories with tables of contents; word lists; about-the-book questions; 64, 80, or 96 pages; short chapters; short paragraphs; and large fonts, then **ALADDIN QUIX** is *definitely* for you!

ALADDIN QUIX: The next step between ready to reads and longer, more challenging chapter books, for readers five to eight years old.

**Read the other books
in the Elf Academy series!**

Trouble in Toyland

Reindeer Games

Elf ACADEMY

HAPPY SANTA DAY!

BY ALAN KATZ

ILLUSTRATED BY
SERNUR IŞIK

ALADDIN QUIX

NEW YORK LONDON TORONTO SYDNEY NEW DELHI

ALADDIN
Simon & Schuster Children's Publishing Division
1230 Avenue of the Americas, New York, New York 10020
First Aladdin QUIX hardcover edition September 2022
Text copyright © 2022 by Simon & Schuster, Inc.
Illustrations copyright © 2022 by Sernur Işik
Also available in an Aladdin QUIX paperback edition.
All rights reserved, including the right of reproduction in whole or in part in any form.
ALADDIN and the related marks and colophon are trademarks of Simon & Schuster, Inc.
For information about special discounts for bulk purchases, please contact
Simon & Schuster Special Sales at 1-866-506-1949 or business@simonandschuster.com.
The Simon & Schuster Speakers Bureau can bring authors to your live event. For more information or to book an event contact the Simon & Schuster Speakers Bureau at 1-866-248-3049 or visit our website at www.simonspeakers.com.
Designed by Tiara Iandiorio
The illustrations for this book were rendered digitally.
The text of this book was set in Archer Medium.
Manufactured in the United States of America 0822 LAK
2 4 6 8 10 9 7 5 3 1
Library of Congress Control Number 2022936582
ISBN 978-1-5344-6795-8 (hc)
ISBN 978-1-5344-6794-1 (pbk)
ISBN 978-1-5344-6796-5 (ebook)

To Karen,
who adds a happy dose of ho ho ho!
—A. K.

Cast of Characters

Santa: Jolly gift giver

Mrs. Claus: The first lady of the North Pole

Molly: One of the reindeer at Reindeer Ranch and twin brother of Wally

Wally: One of the reindeer at Reindeer Ranch and twin brother of Molly

Roger: The rancher at Reindeer Ranch

Ms. Dow: The toy workshop

teacher at Elf Academy

Andy Snowden: An Elf Academy student

Jay: Andy's best friend

Susu: Andy's twin sister

Zahara: An Elf Academy student

Kal: An Elf Academy student

Nicole: Susu's best friend

Principal Evergreen: Principal of Elf Academy

Craig: Andy and Susu's older brother

Contents

1

December 26

It was the morning of the day after Christmas.

Santa's Christmas Eve ride was over, and it had been **magical**. A full moon and bright stars had lit the sky for the last part of the journey, making it easy to see the way back home to the North Pole.

Santa and the reindeer had traveled over thirty-nine million miles to deliver just the right toys to kids everywhere. And even now Santa was . . .

- sleepy.
- tired.
- pooped.

Santa **slumped** in his chair at the kitchen table across from **Mrs. Claus**.

His eyes were half closed. His

head was nodding up and down.

"Maybe you should take a nap," Mrs. Claus suggested.

"That's a . . . *yawn* . . . good . . . *yawn* . . . idea," Santa said. "*Yawn.*"

He stood up, walked over to an overstuffed chair near the living room fireplace, and plopped down in it. He fell asleep faster than a melting snowflake.

"Zzzzzzz . . . zzzzzz . . ."

☆ ☆ ☆

Over at Reindeer Ranch, **Molly**, her twin brother, **Wally**, and the other reindeer were yawning too.

After all, they'd also made quite a trip around the globe helping Santa deliver toys. Flying through the night sky while pulling Santa's heavy **sleigh** was tiring.

Roger, the rancher at Reindeer Ranch, was taking good care of them; he gave each one a soft pillow, a fluffy blanket, and a healthy, leafy green snack.

And faster than two melting snowflakes, they were all asleep.

2

Cleaning Up

Not far away, at the Elf Academy toy workshop, the elves in **Ms. Dow**'s second-grade class were full of energy. Of course, they hadn't traveled with Santa the night before, so they had slept **soundly**.

"Attention, everyone!" announced Ms. Dow. "Your toy making this year was **elf-tastic**, but all the last-minute finishing touches left quite a mess in this workshop. There are ribbons and bows and bells and balls all over the workbenches. And I'm not sure *what* those are on the ceiling."

"Those are the **helium**-filled race cars I built," **Andy Snowden** answered. "They zoom really fast on the floor, but because of the helium, they won't stay *on* the floor!"

"That's why they're on the ceiling!" Andy's best friend, **Jay**, told Ms. Dow with a laugh.

Everyone at Elf Academy, especially Jay, knew that Andy had an imagination as big as the Arctic Ocean. He was always thinking of how he could make something bigger and better and more fun.

"I'm sorry I

asked," Ms. Dow said, frowning. "Now everyone, please gather the items and put them where they belong. That way we can use these leftovers all year long and won't be wasting a single piece."

The elves started picking things up to take to the **storage** bins.

Andy asked

his teacher, "Would you like me to sing the toy cleanup song, Ms. Dow? Maybe it'll help everyone work faster."

"I don't **recall** any song like that, Andy," she replied.

Andy smiled. "That's because I'm singing it for the very first time. Listen . . . ," he said and began:

♪"Pick up one red ribbon;
put it in the bin.
Pick up some tape
and scissors, too,
and do it with a grin."

"Can you believe I just made that up?" Andy asked. "I'll sing it again."

Before Ms. Dow could stop him, Andy started singing the tune over and over again.

"Stop!" Susu, Andy's twin

sister, yelled, putting her hands over her ears. "You're not even on key, Andy! And I can't hear myself think."

But all the elves *did* clean up faster while Andy sang, hoping they could finish before he started all over again.

3

Thanks a Lot!

When all the bows, bells, glitter, crayons, and paint had been put away, Andy finally stopped singing.

Ms. Dow looked around the classroom and said, "You've all cleaned up the workshop very nicely. Your song must have worked, Andy.

"And now, class," she added, "I have another **task** for you."

Andy's friend **Zahara** raised her hand. "What is it?" she asked Ms. Dow.

Ms. Dow began, "As you know, all of us at the North Pole love making children happy. And Santa is so busy making sure each and every gift is delivered **precisely** on time year after year. He gives so much to everyone."

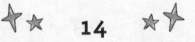

"That's because he's jolly!" Jay called out.

"That's true, Jay," Ms. Dow said. "But while kids write to tell him what gifts they'd like, I don't think very many send him a note to say thank you."

"I never thought about that," Zahara said. "Gee, I wonder if this makes Santa *less* jolly."

The elves couldn't believe it. Could Santa really be sad and not jolly? What could they do?

"Well, *we* should make him a

card," Susu said. "And have every kid in the world sign it."

"Wouldn't that take a lot of time?" **Kal** wondered.

"It would also take up a lot of room," **Nicole** pointed out. "Millions and millions of **signatures**, all on one gigantic card."

Zahara thought about that for a moment. "Well then," she said. "Let's just have the kids sign their *first* names."

Ms. Dow smiled and told the class that a thank-you card *just from the elves* was what she actually had in mind. She suggested that they each write a note, and then those notes could be pasted onto a giant card to give to Santa.

"We can begin right now," she told her students as she handed out paper in rainbow colors to each elf.

Andy agreed it was a super way to thank Santa, but when Ms. Dow gave him an orange piece of paper, he blurted out, **"Wait! Hold it!** I have an even better idea! A really, really great way to say thank you!"

"We are *not* singing Santa a song, Andy," Ms. Dow replied.

"Wouldn't that be awesome, though?" Andy smiled. "But think about it: What's more fun than a card and more fun than a song?"

Kal, Nicole, and Jay each took a guess:

"A new hat for Santa?"

"A pair of fuzzy slippers?"

"A mouthful of chocolate-covered pretzels?"

"No! No! And no!" Andy answered. "I'll give you a **hint:**

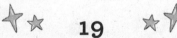

it's a five-letter word, and the first two letters are *P-A*."

Again Kal, Nicole, and Jay each took a guess:

"Pants?"

"Paste?"

"A panda?"

"No! No! And no again!" Andy said. "The word is ***P-A-R-T-Y***."

"What do you mean, Andy?" Zahara wanted to know.

"A party," Andy said. "Let's throw Santa Claus the best and biggest thank-you party!"

4

Surprise!

The elves loved Andy's idea.

Ms. Dow did too.

"I will speak with **Principal Evergreen** and the other Elf Academy teachers before the end of the school day," she told the class. "Maybe we can hold the party first thing tomorrow morning. But we will have to see if Santa is available."

Andy nodded, but then his ears started to tingle, and once again he blurted out, "**Wait! Hold it!** I have an even better idea. . . . Let's make it a *surprise* party!"

Everyone was silent for a moment, and then the entire class, even Ms. Dow, clapped, cheered, and stomped their feet.

The elves made so much noise that:

- a basket of bells tumbled off a bookshelf.
- Ms. Evergreen raced from her office down to the classroom.
- Santa woke up from his nap.

☆ ☆ ☆

Santa stretched a giant stretch and told Mrs. Claus, "I feel quite rested now."

Then he joined his wife for a cup of Mrs. Claus's favorite tea: cranberry candy cane.

As he sipped, Santa said, "We are so very lucky that the Elf Academy students are so talented and **hardworking**. We could never get through the holiday season without them, year after year."

"We are indeed," Mrs. Claus answered. "And don't forget all the help from Principal Evergreen, Ms. Dow, and the rest of the teachers and staff."

Santa stroked his beard. He was silent for a moment and then took another sip of tea. "I wish there were some way I could let them know how much I appreciate them," he said.

"How about sending them a card?" Mrs. Claus suggested.

"That's a very nice thought," Santa said. "But I wonder if there's something even better."

"You could bake a **batch** of your famous North Pole cookies," Mrs. Claus offered, smiling. "After all, no one knows more about cookies than you do."

"That's true. I've tasted thousands and thousands of cookies left for me by kindhearted children," Santa said. "And my North Pole recipe mixes together all the best ones I've ever had."

"Then it's decided," Mrs. Claus said. "We will bake North Pole cookies!"

But then Santa's eyes twinkled. **"Wait! Hold it!** I have an even better idea!" he said. "Think about it: What's more fun than a card and more fun than cookies?"

Mrs. Claus thought for a moment and told Santa that she couldn't think of anything.

"**Ho ho ho!** Here's my idea," he said. "Let's throw the elves a *big thank-you surprise party!*"

5

Party Planning

Usually after lunch the elves never wanted to come in from recess. But today they raced in after a game of Polar Bear tag. **"Ms. Dow! Ms. Dow!"** Jay called out. "Did you talk to others about the surprise party?"

Andy added, "Can we have it? What did Principal Evergreen say?"

For the first time that Andy could remember, Ms. Dow didn't remind him or Jay to raise their hands before asking a question.

She answered, "Yes, class. I'm happy to report that the party is on. Ms. Evergreen has called an assembly now to **assign** the different party jobs. Please line up."

For the first time that Andy

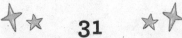

could remember, the elves lined up and walked to the assembly quickly and quietly.

"Welcome!" Ms. Evergreen greeted the elves. "First I would like to thank Ms. Dow's class for this wonderful and well-deserved thank-you for Santa. As the party is tomorrow, we have to move quickly."

She continued, "This afternoon we will all be *very* busy. Grades one and two will make stars. Grades three and four

will blow up the balloons. And grades five and six will make the **streamers**. Once you all return home, the rest of the staff will **decorate** the Sugarplum Toy Storage Building."

"Ms. Evergreen? How will we let Santa know to come to the Sugarplum?" asked Nicole.

"After our assembly," replied Ms. Evergreen, "I will call Santa and Mrs. Claus and tell them to meet us first thing in the morning to discuss an important toy matter. Santa *never* says no to toy matters!"

"Ms. Evergreen," Andy called out. "Ms. Evergreen? What about the Reindeer Ranch reindeer? Can we invite them too?"

"That's another fine idea, Andy," said Ms. Dow.

"Thank you," Andy said. "If it's okay with you and Ms. Evergreen, Jay and I can run over to Reindeer Ranch right now and ask them to join us tomorrow."

A few minutes later, the best

friends rushed through the Reindeer Ranch gates and found their friends. They told Molly and Wally all about the surprise party plans.

"That sounds like such fun," they told the elves.

"It will be," Andy replied. "And of course, you and all the reindeer are invited. So is Roger. But remember, not a word to Santa or Mrs. Claus!"

"Shhh-hhh,"

Andy shushed.

☆ ☆ ☆

Once Andy and Jay were back at Elf Academy, Ms. Evergreen had one last item on her to-do list.

"And finally," Ms. Evergreen said, smiling from ear to ear, "the Elf Academy **chefs** will be baking Santa's favorite cake: peppermint sprinkle swirl. See you all tomorrow for a super Santa surprise!"

PEPPERMINT SPRINKLE SWIRL CAKE RECIPE

MILK

FLOUR

SANTA'S FAVORITE!

by MS. EVERGREEN

6

The Santa Plan

Of course, no one at Elf Academy had any idea that Santa was also making plans.

"I know a great place to hold the party: the Sugarplum Toy Storage Building. It's empty now that all the toys were delivered," Santa said.

"Perfect!" Mrs. Claus said. "You'd better start baking, though. All those elves are sure to **gobble** up lots of cookies."

"You're right!" said Santa. "I hope we have all the cookie **ingredients**."

Just then, *brrrrrrinnnng . . . brrrrinng . . . brrrrinng!* The Claus telephone startled them.

Who could be calling? Santa wondered. *Isn't everyone pooped?*

"Ho ho ho hello?" Santa said.

"Good afternoon, Santa. It's Principal Evergreen. I hope I'm not disturbing you, but first thing tomorrow morning, we need to have a most important toy-making meeting. Please be at the Sugarplum at 9 a.m. sharp."

Santa couldn't believe his luck! "Say no more, Ms. Evergreen. Mrs. Claus and I will meet you at 9 a.m.," he answered, and quickly hung up the phone. Usually a

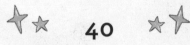

PRINCIPAL
MS. EVERGREEN

toy-making meeting could wait, but Santa was delighted to be told about the one tomorrow.

"Listen to this!" he told Mrs. Claus. "Tomorrow morning all of Elf Academy will be in **attendance** at the Sugarplum. It's the perfect opportunity to surprise them with the thank-you party!"

Mrs. Claus beamed. "That's Santa-rific! Now it's time to start baking!"

☆ ☆ ☆

Andy, Susu, and their older brother, **Craig**, spent the evening telling their parents all about the party for Santa. For the first time their parents could remember, all three of their children wanted to get to sleep early!

Susu said, "The sooner we go to bed, the faster we can surprise Santa!"

Andy thought the party plans sounded elf-tastic. But while Santa liked peppermint sprinkle swirl cake, Andy wasn't sure

it was special enough to *really* thank him.

It was when Andy was brush-ing his teeth that his ears started tingling.

Andy got into bed, puffed his pillows, and lay his head down. Right before he closed his eyes, he knew just what the extra ingredient should be: gumdrops!

Lots and lots and lots of gumdrops!

The only problem? How would Andy decorate the cake *before* the surprise party?

7

Getting Ready

The next morning Andy woke up before his family, quickly got dressed, and zoomed over to Jay's house. He tapped on his friend's bedroom window and **signaled** him to the front door.

"Andy, what are you doing here so early?" Jay asked, peeking his head outside.

"We need to make Santa's surprise cake even more super special," Andy explained as he held up a large bag. "And I have a sweet idea. Get dressed as fast as you can. I'll tell you my gumdrop plan on our way over."

Jay was outside a few moments later, and the friends hurried to the Sugarplum. Andy knew he and his best friend would have to

work fast. Sure, they knew they could **swiftly** build a toy submarine or a birdhouse, but decorate a huge cake in a flash?

☆ ☆ ☆

It almost felt like Christmas morning when the elves arrived at school. They were all so excited and nervous, they could hardly keep still on the way to their classrooms.

"I can't wait to see Santa's face.

I hope we make him super jolly!"
Kal said to Ms. Dow.

"I hope so too, Kal," Ms. Dow
replied.

☆ ☆ ☆

Meanwhile, at the Sugarplum Toy
Storage Building . . .

"Andy, we can't fit another
gumdrop on the cake," Jay said.
"There isn't any space left."

"Just one more gumdrop,
Jay," Andy said, looking up. "I

see room at the tippy top. I just have to figure out a way to reach the . . ."

And then Andy noticed the balloons floating near the ceiling of the room.

"Help me out, Jay!" he called. "If I gather enough of the balloons together, they

can lift me to the top, and I can plop down the last gumdrop."

"Another great idea, Andy!" Jay said. **"Here we go!"**

8

Smooshed!

At 8:59 a.m., everyone from Elf Academy, as well as Reindeer Ranch, stood outside Door A of the Sugarplum building, waiting to go in.

Also at 8:59 a.m., Santa and

Mrs. Claus stood outside Door B of the Sugarplum, waiting to go in. Santa was carrying trays of North Pole cookies piled high. Mrs. Claus held a gigantic bunch of balloons.

And at 9 a.m. on the dot, Doors A and B opened at the **exact** same time. Everyone burst in, and . . .

"SURPRISE! SURPRISE! SURPRISE!"

yelled Andy, who was stuck at the very top of the gumdrop-covered

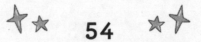

peppermint
sprinkle swirl
cake.

**"SURPRISE!
SURPRISE!
SURPRISE!"**

yelled Jay, who was barely hang-
ing on to the balloons close to the
ceiling.

Santa, Mrs. Claus, Ms. Dow, Principal Evergreen, and the rest of Elf Academy couldn't believe their eyes.

"Andy!" shouted Craig. "What are you doing?"

"Jay, how did you ever get up there?" screamed Kal.

"Andy Snowden! Jay Fir! Come down from there immediately," yelled Ms. Dow.

"Everything is ruined!" cried Nicole. **"Everything!"**

Mrs. Claus saw how upset

everyone was. "Nicole," she asked, "what do you mean by 'everything is ruined'?"

"Santa, Mrs. Claus, we were throwing you a surprise party to thank you for all that you do for everyone," explained Andy. "But Santa, what are you doing with those cookies? And balloons?"

Santa looked at Mrs. Claus.

Mrs. Claus looked at Santa.

"Let's rescue Andy and Jay first and then we'll explain," Mrs. Claus told the crowd. "Molly and

58

Wally, would you please fly up and get the boys?"

Molly flew up to the cake and **steadied** herself while Andy climbed out, covered in icing, crumbs, and a few orange gumdrops. It was easier for Jay to just jump onto Wally's back.

When the elves were back on the ground and Andy had **toweled** off, Santa started talking.

"Mrs. Claus and I thank you for such a thoughtful surprise. We are a wonderful North Pole

family, aren't we?" he said.

Everyone nodded.

"Mrs. Claus and I had the same plans as you: we wanted to thank you for all the hard and kind work *you* do for children all over the world."

"*Two* parties at the same time?" Roger asked. **"This is fantastic!"**

"Except—look at the cake," said Susu. "How are we supposed to eat that mess?"

The peppermint sprinkle swirl

gumdrop cake did look sort of smooshed and smashed and soggy.

"Well," Andy began, "I knew it just needed something extra

elf special to thank Santa. And I was sure gumdrops would do the trick."

"They did the trick all right, Andy, and not the treat," said Mrs. Claus, and she began laughing so hard she couldn't stop. And once she started laughing, the whole room joined her. Even the reindeer.

"You are right, Andy. Gumdrops are one of my favorites," Santa told him. "Thanks to you and Jay for making the extra-special effort."

Santa winked at Andy and continued, "I don't know about any of you, but I think cake tastes delicious no matter how smooshed it may be."

"And I say it's time to get our two no-longer-surprise parties started," Principal Evergreen added.

"Well, what are we waiting for?" Santa boomed. **"Let's have a jolly good time!"**

And a jolly good time was had by all.

Word List

assign (ah•SIHN): To give a specific task or job to

attendance (ah•TEN•dehnce): Number of people in a place

batch (BATCH): A group of things or people

chefs (SHEFS): Professional cooks

decorate (DECK•or•eight): Make more beautiful by design

exact (eggs•ACT): Completely correct

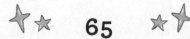

gobble (GAH•bull): Eat and swallow food quickly

hardworking: (HARD WER•khing: Putting a lot of effort into a job

helium (HEE•lee•um): Colorless gas that is lighter than air, used to fill balloons

hint (HINT): Suggest something

ingredients (in•GREE•dee•entz): Some of the things used to make food

magical (MAH•jih•kul): Very exciting, filled with wonder

66

precisely (pree•SEIS•lee): Exactly

recall (ree•CALL): Remember something

signaled (SIG•nuhld): Movement or action that gave information

signatures (SIG•nah•chures): People's written names

sleigh (SLAY): Large open vehicle usually pulled by a strong animal

slumped (SLUMPT): Sank down heavily

soundly (SOUND•lee): In a deep state

steadied (STED•eed): Held firmly

storage (STORE•ahge): Space where you put things that are not in use

streamers (STREEM•ehrs): Long and narrow pieces of paper used as decoration

swiftly (SWIFT•lee): Move quickly

task (TASK): Small job

toweled (TOW•uhld): Dried off with a towel

Questions

1. Why were Santa and the reindeer so tired on December 26?

2. What is the best surprise you have ever received?

3. What's the best surprise you've ever given someone?

4. Think of three fun ways you can say thank you to someone.

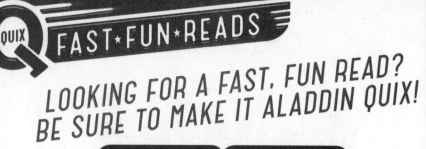